We only have one home.
And if home is really where the heart is, then
let's fill every corner of our Little Blue Planet with love.

This book is made with 100% renewable resources and dedicated to you,

_____

Your Name

First U.S. Edition, published in 2019 by Avocado Green Mattress®
12 Hudson Place, Suite 100, Hoboken, NJ 07030
Printed in the United States by Imago
Text and illustration copyright © 2019 by Avocado Green Mattress & The Mill
Book design by The Mill for Avocado Green Mattress
Written by Anaïs La Rocca and Eve Grissinger
Illustrations by Wendy Eduarte and Syd Fini
All rights reserved
ISBN 978-0-578-53595-1
WWW.AVOCADOGREENMATTRESS.COM

THE
Little
Blue Planet

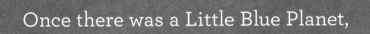
Once there was a Little Blue Planet,

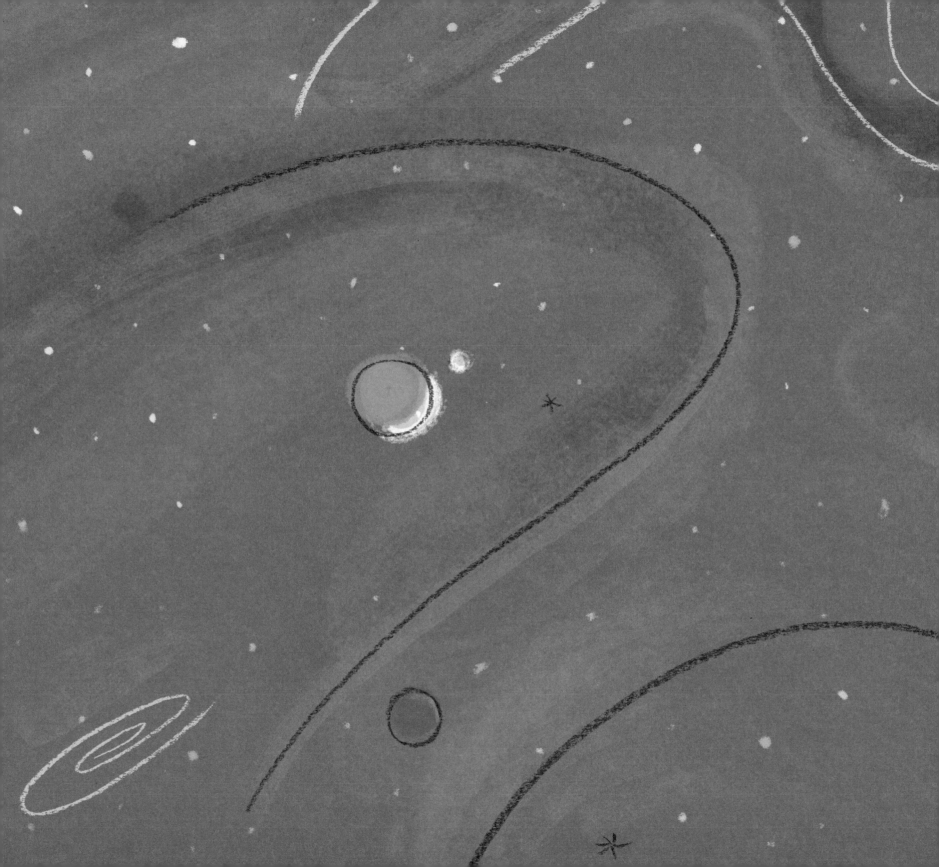

that didn't seem so little when you stood on it.

In fact, many thought it was endless, filled with plentiful resources.

And the Little Blue Planet was proud to be able to give so much.

Life was so
wonderful on
the Little
Blue Planet.

But soon,

the people started to forget
to take care of it.

Over time, the Little Blue Planet
got a little less blue, and a little less green,

and a little more gray.

But the people didn't notice.

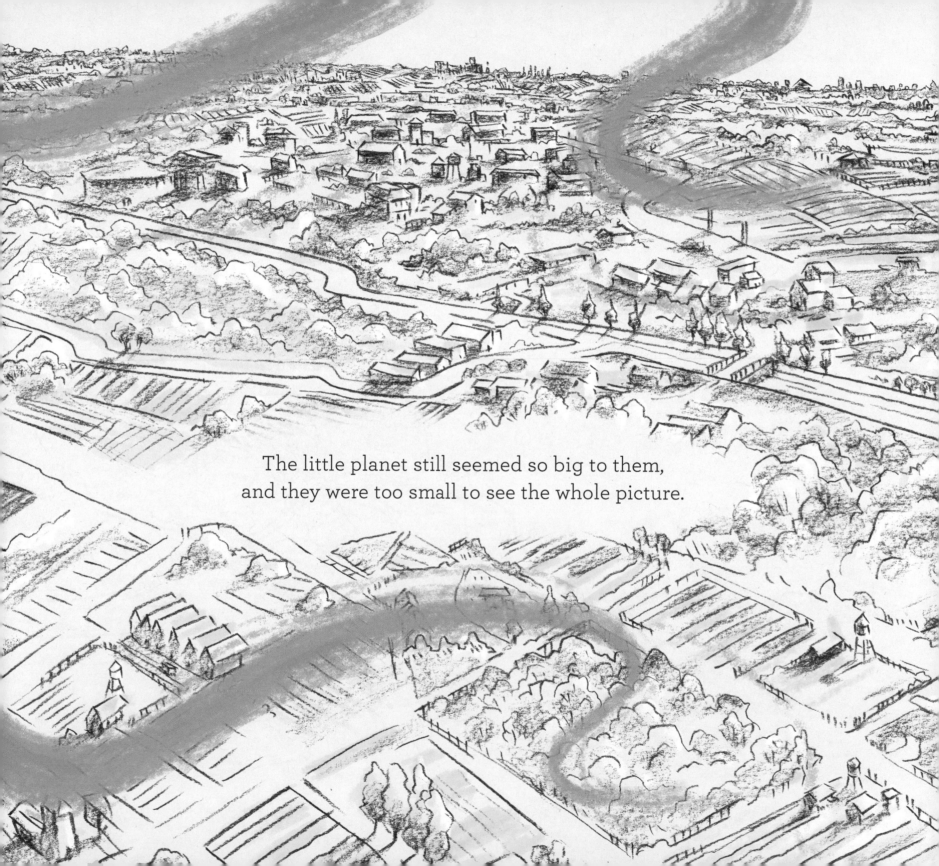

The little planet still seemed so big to them,
and they were too small to see the whole picture.

So the planet tried to show them.

It changed
its weather, its air,
and its oceans.

And then, the people began to notice.

We realized the Little Blue Planet
could only take care of us,
if we took care of it.

So we started to.

We started to treat the oceans, and the forests,
and the great big sky like what they are: our home.

This isn't just any story.

It's a story that we're all a part of, every day.

And now we know, to take care of each other,

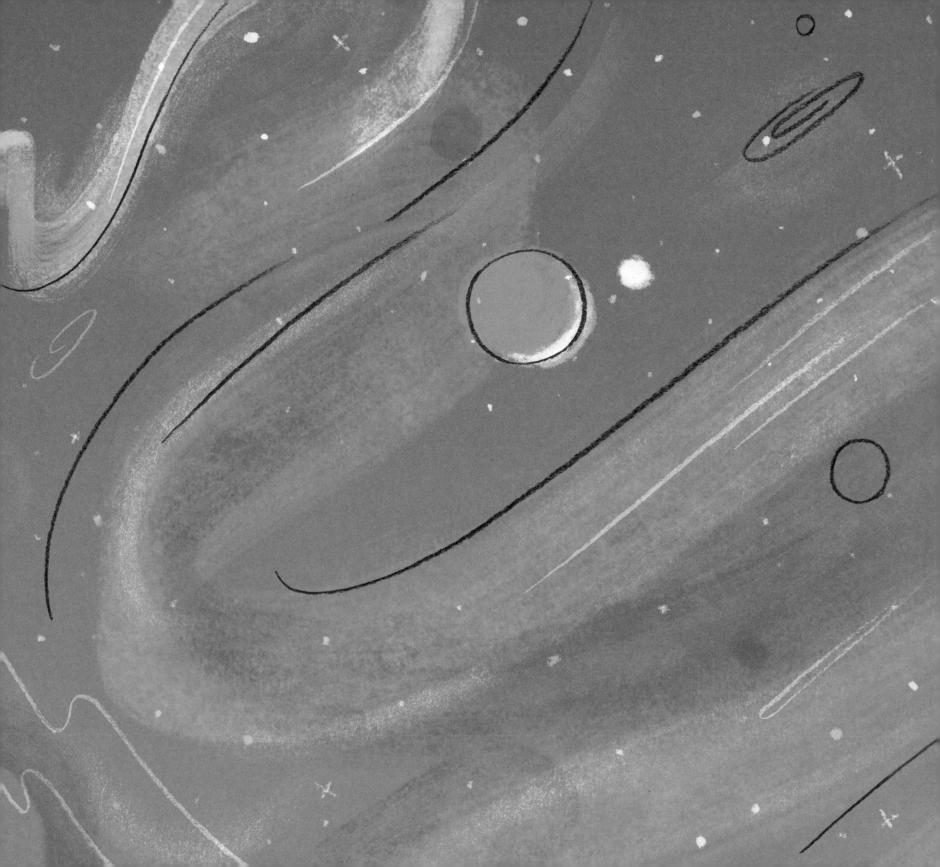

we must first take care of our Little Blue Planet.

100% of the net proceeds of this book go to 1% For The Planet®.
Because the biggest nightmare is waking up to
a world that we've taken for granted.